Acting Edition

I0591741

Tomorrow Game

by Brandy N. Carie

Copyright © 2023 by Brandy N. Carie
All Rights Reserved

TOMORROW GAME is fully protected under the copyright laws of the
United States of America, the British Commonwealth, including Canada,
and all member countries of the Berne Convention for the Protection of
Literary and Artistic Works, the Universal Copyright Convention, and/
or the World Trade Organization conforming to the Agreement on Trade
Related Aspects of Intellectual Property Rights. All rights, including
professional and amateur stage productions, recitation, lecturing, public
reading, motion picture, radio broadcasting, television, online/digital
production, and the rights of translation into foreign languages are
strictly reserved.

ISBN 978-0-573-71048-3

www.concordtheatricals.com
www.concordtheatricals.co.uk

FOR PRODUCTION INQUIRIES

UNITED STATES AND CANADA
info@concordtheatricals.com
1-866-979-0447

UNITED KINGDOM AND EUROPE
licensing@concordtheatricals.co.uk
020-7054-7298

Each title is subject to availability from Concord Theatricals Corp.,
depending upon country of performance. Please be aware that
TOMORROW GAME may not be licensed by Concord Theatricals
Corp. in your territory. Professional and amateur producers should
contact the nearest Concord Theatricals Corp. office or licensing
partner to verify availability.

CAUTION: Professional and amateur producers are hereby warned that
TOMORROW GAME is subject to a licensing fee. The purchase, renting,
lending or use of this book does not constitute a license to perform this
title(s), which license must be obtained from Concord Theatricals Corp.
prior to any performance. Performance of this title(s) without a license is
a violation of federal law and may subject the producer and/or presenter
of such performances to civil penalties. Both amateurs and professionals
considering a production are strongly advised to apply to the appropriate
agent before starting rehearsals, advertising, or booking a theatre. A
licensing fee must be paid whether the title(s) is presented for charity
or gain and whether or not admission is charged. Professional/Stock
licensing fees are quoted upon application to Concord Theatricals Corp.

This work is published by Samuel French, an imprint of Concord
Theatricals Corp.

No one shall make any changes in this title(s) for the purpose of production. No part of this book may be reproduced, stored in a retrieval system, scanned, uploaded, or transmitted in any form, by any means, now known or yet to be invented, including mechanical, electronic, digital, photocopying, recording, videotaping, or otherwise, without the prior written permission of the publisher. No one shall share this title(s), or any part of this title(s), through any social media or file hosting websites.

For all inquiries regarding motion picture, television, online/digital and other media rights, please contact Concord Theatricals Corp.

MUSIC AND THIRD-PARTY MATERIALS USE NOTE

Licensees are solely responsible for obtaining formal written permission from copyright owners to use copyrighted music and/or other copyrighted third-party materials (e.g. artworks, logos) in the performance of this play and are strongly cautioned to do so. If no such permission is obtained by the licensee, then the licensee must use only original music and materials that the licensee owns and controls. Licensees are solely responsible and liable for clearances of all third-party copyrighted materials, including without limitation music, and shall indemnify the copyright owners of the play(s) and their licensing agent, Concord Theatricals Corp., against any costs, expenses, losses and liabilities arising from the use of such copyrighted third-party materials by licensees. For music, please contact the appropriate music licensing authority in your territory for the rights to any incidental music.

IMPORTANT BILLING AND CREDIT REQUIREMENTS

If you have obtained performance rights to this title, please refer to your licensing agreement for important billing and credit requirements.

Use of the excerpt from *Deep Survival*, by Laurence Gonzales has been reproduced by kind permission of the author.

The author is indebted to a production of *TOMORROW GAME*'s initial scene during Houston's 2017 Future is Female Festival, without which the full-length script could not have come to be. This production was directed by Dana Bowman. The cast was as follows:

BELL..Shunté Lofton
ROE...Jasmine Thomas

TOMORROW GAME was supported in its development by a 2017 Edward Albee Foundation Fellowship. In conjunction with a 2018 KCACTF Steinberg Award, an excerpt of the play received a 2019 staged reading at the Kennedy Center, directed by Laley Lippard. The cast was as follows:

BELL..Regina Aquino
ROE................................. Moriamo Temidayo Akibu

TOMORROW GAME was further developed in Barter Theatre's 2020 Appalachian Festival of Plays and Playwrights and presented in a digital staged reading directed by Nicholas Piper. The cast was as follows:

BELL..Kim Morgan Dean
ROE...Paris Bradstreet

CHARACTERS

BELL – Female. Small. Whip smart but careful not to show it off. Gifted is not a thing anymore. Calculating but also sometimes impulsive. Tough but not that strong. A good liar. Lonesome.

ROE – Female. Physically imposing. Not chatty but she is paying attention. Instinctive, careful. Athletes are not a thing anymore. Strong but only sometimes tough. A bad liar. Lonesome.

SETTING

The former continental United States.
Somewhere with trees that used to look different.

TIME

After.

AUTHOR'S NOTES

THE EARTH

This is a world of profound solitude and constant danger. The dangerous things are also beautiful. Infrastructure is gone, order is mythic, no one believes that help is coming. Most people can't imagine a world where help just *comes*. There is no cure for the sickly earth, no place of refuge to quest toward. Just death, and not-death, not yet, not today.

ON LANGUAGE & SONG

The women in this play have been mostly alone. They speak in the shorthand of familiarity they learned when the only people around them were familiar. They say nothing that doesn't need to be said. People who speak to fill the void are not the kind of people who survive. Bell's song is also not sung to fill the void; it is a mnemonic device that helps map her surroundings.

ON PUNCTUATION

A slash /in the text indicates an overlap where the next line begins.
A question that ends with a period indicates no upward inflection. (Do you think the speaker already knows the answer.)
A sentence without concluding punctuation is one where the speaker has more to say.

ON CASTING

Both performers may be any age between twenty and fifty. Both performers may be any race. However, anything that might impose a sense of inequality between them (i.e. a major age disparity, or casting one white and one Black performer) should be avoided. The biggest differences between them are: Bell is small and Roe is big; Bell is analytic and Roe is emotional; Bell reads books and plays games and lives for tomorrow while Roe watches, listens, and remembers.

STORIES AND BIBLE VERSES

The text read by Bell on page 32 is selected lines from the book of Job, in the New King James Version of the Bible. The stories in Roe's book are my own, to whatever extent that's possible.

"Each man must do his own surviving. He may do it by rescuing someone else, by not being a victim, but just as only he can live his life, so too his survival cannot be shared. No one can do it for him. Privacy is important for strength in that lonely work."
– *Deep Survival*, by Laurence Gonzales

Yesterday

(The setting sun glares blindingly through a large metal door as it is slammed shut by **ROE** *in a gas mask. She locks the door with three heavy locks, one, two, three.)*

(After the sun the room is dim: a cave. A bunker. Large, round-ish. A straw mattress in a corner. Guns on one wall. One whole wall is just stacks of rusty food cans.)

*(***ROE*** is carrying a twisted metal trap. She drops it with a crash.)*

(There are candles lit. A fire in the center of the room, smoldering. Two wooden stools.)

(She takes off the gas mask. She hangs it up next to two other masks. She straightens the other two masks.)

*(***ROE*** looks around the empty room.)*

*(***ROE*** stokes the fire. She sets meat on a spit over the fire.)*

*(***ROE*** takes off a few layers of clothing and hangs them up. Underneath is something comfortable and worn.)*

*(***ROE*** collects the trap and sits by the fire. She studies the trap. A broken hinge?)*

(She gets a toolbox full of tools and random metal doodads. She fiddles.)

*(After a moment, **ROE** peeks at the meat again. Pokes it. Considers, shakes her head. Not yet.)*

*(**ROE** cocks her head, as if listening.)*

*(**ROE** shakes her head, smiling.)*

*(**ROE** fiddles with the trap. She puts a little grease on a rag, and oils it.)*

*(**ROE** looks at the meat again. Now.)*

*(**ROE** eats the meat.)*

ROE. Traps: one set, two set, three set, four set, five set, six broke,

> *(**ROE** whacks the broken trap.)*

seven set, eight set, nine set.

Meat: ...one large animal.

Cans: plenty.

Guns: oiled.

Wood: three trees.

Bucket: empty.

Water: clean.

Patrol: nothing.

Roe: whole.

Winston:

*(**ROE**'s face screws up. She is overwhelmed. We do not cry here. **ROE** gets her shit together.)*

And the evening and the morning were the third day.

(Lights out.)

Yesterday (Again)

(Door closed, candles and fire lit, meat on the spit.)

*(**ROE** does pullups. Drops off the pullup bar. Smiles a little.)*

ROE. Fifty.

(She frowns.)

*(**ROE** takes the meat off the spit. Looks at it.)*

Eat. Eat of my body.

(She looks at the meat.)

EAT!!

Do this in remembrance of me.

*(**ROE** looks at the meat.)*

*(**ROE** eats.)*

Traps: one set, two set, three set, four set, five set, six broke,

*(**ROE** whacks the broken trap.)*

seven set, eight set, nine set.

Meat: ...

*(**ROE** suddenly stands and picks up the nearest object: the trap.)*

(She uses the full force of her body to hurl the trap against a wall.)

(It breaks into many pieces.)

(She blows out the candles.)

And the evening and the morning were the sixth day.

(Lights out.)

Yesterday (Again)

*(**ROE** eats meat by the fire.)*

*(**ROE** finishes the meat.)*

*(**ROE** tinkers with the trap.)*

(There! It's fixed.)

*(**ROE** sets the fixed trap by the door.)*

*(**ROE** picks up the trap and looks at it again.)*

*(**ROE** sets it down.)*

*(**ROE** does pullups. One, Two... **ROE** drops down.)*

*(**ROE** walks in a circle around the whole cave.)*

(Then again. Again, faster.)

*(**ROE** stops in front of the fire and stares at it.)*

ROE. And he said unto them:

A broken trap's a useless trap.

Double check, then check again.

Red sky at night, door stays closed.

Meat first, then cans.

Bored is alive.

Bored is alive.

"Oh that you would appoint me a set time...

And remember me."

>   (**ROE** *picks up the nearest thing: a wooden
>   stool.*)

>   (*She smashes it on the ground, over and over,
>   until it is splinters.*)

>   (*She breathes deeply and feeds the splinters
>   into the fire.*)

And the evening and the morning were the thirty-fourth day.

>   (*Lights.*)

Today

(**BELL** *walks along a grassy path, wearing a gas mask, humming cheerfully. The countryside, but the hint of a small city not too far off. If there are clouds they're tinged with unnatural colors. If we can see details of the city, it is largely a ruin.*)

BELL. *(Singing/humming. Upbeat.)*
SINGING DANDY WHERE DID YOU GO,
WHERE WILL WE GO ...
HMM HMM HMM ...
TOGETHER IN A CITY WITH PURPLE CLOUDS ...

(*She suddenly stoops to look at a patch of tiny yellow flowers on the side of the road.*)

What's this? Safe or not safe...

(**BELL** *examines the flowers closely, then lifts the mask. A moment where she checks – am I dead from breathing the air? Not dead. She leans down toward a flower. She sniffs it. She sticks out her tongue & gives the flower a tiny lick.*)

Not dead yet...
... *SINGING DANDY WHERE DID YOU GO,*
HMMM HMMM FLOWERS OF GOLD
... *HMM HMM FLOWERS OF –*

(**BELL** *plucks the flowers and drops them in her satchel.* **ROE** *enters, wearing a gas mask, carrying a gun.*)

ROE. What you got there.

BELL. *(Careful.)* Little yellow flowers, looks like.

ROE. That so.

BELL. –

ROE. What you planning to do with 'em.

BELL. Eat them. With greens. To add sweetness.

ROE. *(Extremely surprised.) Greens?*

BELL. Yes.

ROE. You got vegetables.

BELL. Yes.

ROE. *Safe* ones? Not contaminated?

BELL. Well I'm still here.

ROE. How you know *those*'re safe?

BELL. Smell, mostly. The color. I can't be sure, of course.

ROE. *(This woman is insane.)* But you'll... you'll eat them just the same.

BELL. I will. With radishes. And dandelion. And vinegar.

ROE. You got *radishes*.

BELL. I do.

ROE. Where. *How.*

BELL. I grew them.

ROE. In the earth.

BELL. In dirt.

   (Pause.)

ROE. This is my area.

BELL. *(She's been waiting for this.)* I'm sorry I saw no sign.

ROE. Don't gotta put one up for it to be mine.

BELL. Of course. I simply mean that I couldn't have known it was yours when I first entered it.

ROE. Now you know.

BELL. Yes.

ROE. You're still on it.

BELL. Shall I go?

ROE. You're on my area.

BELL. You said.

ROE. So I can do what I want.

BELL. You can.

ROE. So

BELL. What is it you want to do?

(**ROE** *raises the gun.*)

ROE. I'm hungry.

BELL. As am I. Quite hungry. Perhaps I'll just go eat.

ROE. Meat's running low.

BELL. I'm very sorry to hear that.

ROE. How'd you grow them vegetables though.

BELL. ...Maybe that's something we could discuss if you put down the gun.

ROE. *(Surprised.)* This is my area.

BELL. Yes.

ROE. I can do what I want.

BELL. *(A bit irritated at this point.) Yes.* But so can I. And I don't want to talk about vegetables when you are pointing a gun at me.

ROE. *This is my –*

BELL. Yes I *know* it is your area and if you are going to shoot then shoot. I will not tell you about my radishes with you pointing a gun at me and I am bored of this repetitive talk!

ROE. I wanna know about them vegetables.

BELL. You surely can't be this stupid. Were you left outside without a mask as a child?

> (**ROE** *lowers the gun.*)

ROE. I'm not stupid.

BELL. No?

ROE. –

BELL. Are you going to shoot me or do you want to hear about the radishes?

ROE. Tell me about the radishes. Then I'll shoot you.

BELL. No.

> (**BELL** *begins to walk away.* **ROE** *shoots in the air.* **BELL** *jumps but continues walking away.*)

ROE. Hey! *HEY!* Not shooting.

> (**BELL** *slowly turns.*)

BELL. You're not?

ROE. I'm putting the gun down.

BELL. Over there.

ROE. ...Over there.

BELL. Good.

ROE. So.

BELL. I dug the earth from high ground after a clean rain and I put it in a wooden box. I grow the radishes in the box and I cover the box when the rain is bad. I catch clean rain in a barrel and I use it to water the radishes. And the carrots. And beans.

ROE. Beans!

BELL. Yes.

ROE. But – the little flowers.

BELL. Yes?

ROE. They're...on the ground. They get all the rain. The bad rain, too.

BELL. Yes

ROE. But you eat it anyway.

BELL. It hasn't rained in a week.

ROE. –

BELL. I'm taking a risk.

ROE. You wanna die?

BELL. No.

ROE. Then –

BELL. It's just a risk. It's just a risky game I play. Each day I try a new thing and I say, safe or not safe? And I guess. And If I guess right, then I live. And I eat sweet yellow flowers with my greens. And if I guess wrong, I get sick and I probably die. It's a game. And so far, I'm winning. Perfect score.

ROE. A game?

BELL. *(Sadly.)* Yes, a game. Like Scrabble. I used to be very good at Scrabble.

ROE. Scrabble.

> *(This makes* **BELL** *extremely sad, but we don't cry here.)*

BELL. I have no one to play with anymore. My mother went out in the bad rains. My sister lost her game.

ROE. I –

BELL. I'm going to go now.

> *(Turns to leave.)*

ROE. I want to play a game.

BELL. What?

ROE. I want to play a game.

BELL. You do.

ROE. Yes.

BELL. It could be risky.

ROE. OK.

BELL. ...OK. Take off your mask.

ROE. *(Fearful.)* Is this the game?

BELL. It's how the game begins. *(Beat.)* Take off your mask.

ROE. I'm afraid.

BELL. It's a scary game.

ROE. Are you going to play, too?

BELL. I will.

ROE. ...OK.

BELL. *(Slowly, like a poem.)* Take off your mask. Slowly. Feel the wind ruffle the hairs around your face that are damp from sweat. Feel the breeze dry the sweat on your forehead, your upper lip.

> (**ROE** *is nervous at first, and averts her eyes, but slowly she begins to enjoy the game. She takes off her mask.* **BELL** *moves with*

> *deliberation and joy. She is unafraid. She*
> *has played this game many times before.)*

Look up. The sun is bright. See the clouds. Feel the warmth and the breeze and the clear sky. Take a deep breath. Taste the air. There is perfume. There are yellow flowers. There is green. Somewhere, you can hear a bird. Listen. Look. This is the world without a mask. It is beautiful. It might kill you. How long will you stay?

> *(They stand, still, open, breathing, listening.*
> **ROE** *is full of a rapt wild terrified joy, like*
> *jumping off a cliff into the water far below,*
> *bracing for the impact, hoping it never comes.*
> *Birds chirp. A cloud passes over. They wait.)*

Tomorrow

(**BELL** *is walking along the same path, singing, watching. Her gas mask is handy but not on.*)

BELL.

FOUR LEGS OR THREE, NEVER GET OLD,
FEATHERS OF GREEN, FLOWERS OF GOLD,
SINGING DANDY, WHERE DID YOU GO?
WHERE WILL WE –

(*A gunshot. Not far off.*)

(**BELL** *crouches in the grass, almost hidden.*)

(**ROE** *enters. Gun over her shoulder. Her gas mask and clothes are smeared with blood. Mostly it seems to be her own blood from a big gash on her arm.*)

(**BELL** *comes out from hiding.*)

ROE. You're back in my area.

BELL. Hello

ROE. You sing too loud.

BELL. I like to sing.

(**ROE** *snorts.*)

ROE. What do you want? You wanna get killed?

BELL. No thank you.

Who'd you shoot?

ROE. ....Just an animal.

BELL. Food.

(**ROE** *shrugs.*)

ROE. You're back. In my area.

BELL. You're hurt.

ROE. *You're back. In my –*

BELL. This again?!

ROE. It's still mine

BELL. I thought we... understood each other

ROE. What's there to understand.

BELL. We played a game together

ROE. And.

BELL. So it was... amicable –

ROE. – So that doesn't mean you get to come in my area any time.

BELL. OK. I just...thought. You might have more little yellow flowers.

ROE. My area. My flowers.

BELL. I brought radishes. To trade.

ROE. Radishes!

BELL. But I don't see any flowers.

ROE. ...I ate 'em all.

BELL. Then I guess I will have to keep the radishes.

(**ROE** *raises her gun.*)

ROE. No.

BELL. Oh for rot's sake.

ROE. You're on my area.

BELL. I thought we discussed how I feel about having a gun pointed at me.

ROE. You took flowers *last* time.

(*Pause.* **BELL** *considers.*)

BELL. ...OK. You're right.

ROE. I know.

BELL. Put that thing down. And you can have...four radishes.

ROE. How many you got?

BELL. ...Four.

(**ROE** *suspiciously puts the gun down.*)

Over there –

ROE. Over there, over there, fine.

(**ROE** *puts the gun over there.* **BELL** *gives* **ROE** *four radishes.*)

BELL. I can bring you beans, too –

ROE. Beans!

BELL. But only if you have something to trade.

ROE. Flowers

BELL. No

ROE. There'll be more flowers soon.

BELL. I don't want flowers.

ROE. Why not.

BELL. Flowers don't fill up my belly.

ROE. What then.

BELL. A gun.

(*Pause.*)

ROE. ...Only got one gun.

BELL. Meat, then.

ROE. ...Meat's better than beans.

BELL. I'll bring carrots, too.

> (**ROE** *thinks. She takes a stick, or her fingers, and draws two circles in the dirt, one about half the size of the other. She points to the smaller circle.*)

ROE. This much meat.

> (*She points to the bigger circle.*)

For this much beans.

> (**BELL** *re-draws the meat circle to make it bigger.*)

BELL. This much meat.

ROE. No.

BELL. I'll bring the beans and...

Three carrots.

ROE. ...OK.

Tomorrow.

BELL. There might be a storm tomorrow.

ROE. Might eat your meat tomorrow.

> (**BELL** *nods at* **ROE***'s bleeding cut.*)

BELL. You might die of that tomorrow.

ROE. No.

BELL. –

ROE. Might need extra meat to help me heal.

Might not have any left for you.

Might get real hungry –

BELL. Fine.

Tomorrow.

>　　*(She begins to exit.)*

ROE. Wait.

BELL. Yes?

ROE. I want...another game.

BELL. ...Tomorrow.

>　　*(**BELL** begins to exit. Pauses and looks around warily. Sniffs the air. Dons her gas mask. Exits.)*

Tomorrow

*(There is a gathering darkness. **BELL** enters, heavily layered, head to toe. Her mask is securely on.)*

BELL. Hey! Beans and carrots! Hey! I'm here to trade!

*(**BELL** looks around.)*

(Shouting.) FLOWERS OF GOLD, WHERE DID YOU GO, HEY! Beans, cunt! Beans and suckclit carrots!

*(**ROE** enters, fearful, in a heavy jacket and mask.)*

ROE. *(Whispers.)* Quietfuckquiet! There's animals around.

BELL. I came like you asked.

ROE. Shouldn't've

BELL. Where's my meat?

ROE. Storm's coming fast

BELL. I want my meat.

ROE. It's at my place.

BELL. OK. Let's go there.

ROE. You can't go to my place.

BELL. I want my meat. There's a storm coming. Even so, I brought beans and carrots to trade, today, like you asked.

ROE. Give them to me.

BELL. Not until I get my meat.

*(**ROE** points her gun.)*

ROE. Give them to me.

BELL. *(Done with this shit.)* Get that thing out of my face or I'll never bring you another bean or show you another game.

NOW!

> (**ROE** *lowers the weapon.*)

That's no way to treat someone who brings you food before a bad storm.

ROE. It's a fair trade.

BELL. I won't know that until I get my meat. At your place.

We need to go before the rain comes.

ROE. ...This way.

> *(There is a soft sizzling sound.* **BELL** *looks down to her shoulder and sees a drop has fallen there, slowly burning.)*

BELL. Faster

> (**ROE** *looks up at the sky and begins to run.* **BELL** *follows. Another drop hits and another. Sizzle. Sizzle. The slow beginning of a heavy storm. Darkness. Through the dark the sound of a metal latch, a heavy door opens and slams closed.)*

Later

> *(Inside **ROE**'s place. It is unlit. We can hear them fumbling in the dark. **ROE** turns on a flashlight. She locks the three inside locks. **BELL** strips off her clothing.)*

BELL. You have *batteries?*

> *(**ROE** doesn't answer. She moves around the room lighting candles. As soon as one or two are lit she turns off the flashlight and stows it away. **ROE** strips off her clothing.)*
>
> *(After they are down to their underwear they stop and look at each other. They really look.)*
>
> *(They each have raw red acid burns on their shoulders, necks, and arms. **ROE** takes a large bucket of water and splashes it carefully on her burns. She hands the bucket to **BELL**, who does the same.)*
>
> *(**ROE** goes back to lighting candles. Then she lights the fire.)*

Is that safe?

ROE. The cave goes up and out. Smoke comes out a mile or so south.

BELL. How do you have batteries?

ROE. ...Only for emergencies.

> *(**BELL** looks around. She is particularly interested in the wall of food cans. And even more interested in the four guns hanging by the door.)*

BELL. You said you only have one gun.

ROE. ...No bullets for those.

BELL. –

> (**BELL** *still has her bag slung over her shoulder, over her underwear. She checks inside it to see that the beans and carrots are intact. **ROE** gingerly picks up her clothes from the floor and inspects them. They have holes. They're wet. Sighing, she hangs them by the fire to dry.)*

> (**BELL** *takes her own clothes and hangs them up as well. **ROE** places her gas mask and **BELL***'s *gas mask next to the other two on the wall. She goes to a chest and finds new, unburnt clothes to put on.)*

Do you have something I can wear?

ROE. For trade?

BELL. Hospitality. Until my clothes are dry.

ROE. What will you give me.

BELL. That's not what hospitality means.

ROE. So?

...You can bring something later.

BELL. –

> (*Outside we can distantly hear heavy rain. There is a shock of thunder, like an explosion.)*

Lightning

ROE. Don't touch the door. Metal.

> (**ROE** *hands **BELL** a large man's shirt to put on.)*

Storm could last for days

BELL. I suppose it could. Or it could clear up tomorrow.

ROE. Maybe

> (**ROE** *places a pot over the fire. She goes to the
> corner, where there is a large flat stone on the
> floor, and lifts it to reveal a dark opening.
> She reaches her arm deep into the hole in
> the ground and pulls out a packet wrapped
> in burlap and twine.* **ROE** *looks up and sees*
> **BELL** *watching.*)

Meat

BELL. It's...cool? In there?

ROE. Cold.

BELL. Brilliant. Did you build...all this?

ROE. My grampa did

BELL. Is he –

ROE. Gone

BELL. I'm sorry.

ROE. –

BELL. Do you want to make a stew? I have the beans, and
the carrots.

ROE. MY beans and carrots –

BELL. Is that *my* meat?

ROE. ...Yes

BELL. Then we should put it all in the same pot and make
a stew. It will taste good and it will feed us both. Fair.

ROE. ...Alright

BELL. Is there a knife?

ROE. –

BELL. For cutting the carrots?

>   (**ROE** *pulls a large knife from a sheath on her
>   ankle.* **BELL** *reaches for it.* **ROE** *pushes* **BELL**
>   *aside and chops the carrots, dropping them
>   in the pot with the beans. Eventually she also
>   adds the meat.*)

Do you have...seasonings? Onion?

ROE. I have meat

BELL. ...What's in all those cans?

ROE. *(Shrugging.)* Food

BELL. How did you get so many?

ROE. Looked for them. Found them. Brought them back
here.

>   (*Looking up at the stack of cans,* **BELL** *gasps.*)

BELL. You have Coke!

ROE. Coke

BELL. It's a – it's not food, it's a drink.

>   (**ROE** *stares at her.*)

It's from...before. I had it once. It was sweet but also...
like nothing else.

ROE. Coke

BELL. You should try it

>   (**ROE** *looks up at the stacks of cans.*)

ROE. Which one is it?

BELL. It says "Coke" on it. In red letters.

>   (*Pause.*)

ROE. You get it.

(*The Coke is high on the wall.* **BELL** *climbs precariously onto a stool, reaches on her tiptoes, and just snags the can.*)

BELL. Ha!

(**ROE** *looks at the can. Opens it. Smells it suspiciously.*)

ROE. You first.

(**BELL** *smells it. She takes a long drink. She smiles a big satisfied smile.*)

BELL. It's good.

(**ROE** *tastes it. She grins. She takes a big gulp.*)

ROE. It is good. It's good!

We can put it in the stew.

BELL. Maybe just a little bit.

(**ROE** *pours a small amount of the coke in the stew pot. Looks at* **BELL.** **BELL** *nods.* **ROE** *drinks the rest of the coke in one long swig.*)

Oh.

(**ROE** *burps, satisfied, then goes over to a bar near the ceiling and does rapid pull-ups, as an expression of her satisfaction. She jumps down and stretches.*)

ROE. You want to try?

BELL. ...No thanks.

ROE. You can.

BELL. Not right now.

ROE. You try

BELL. I don't want to

ROE. *You try.*

BELL. ...OK.

>   (**BELL** *goes up to the pull-up bar. Takes a deep breath. Jumps up to grab it and struggling, pulls herself up, once. She hangs there for a moment. Then drops down.*)

ROE. ...You're weak.

BELL. I'm better at other things.

>   (**ROE** *jumps up and does more pull-ups.*)

ROE. You're weak and little. I'm strong.

BELL. Clearly.

ROE. Ha!

BELL. But you can't grow radishes

ROE. ...You told me how

BELL. Do you have seeds?

ROE. You'll give me seeds

BELL. No

ROE. Give me seeds

BELL. Maybe. But you'd have to trade. Trade *Big*.

ROE. Trade what?

BELL. A gun.

ROE. I said. No bullets.

BELL. Swamprot.

ROE. I *said* –

BELL. Fine. Let me know when you change your mind. Let me know when you want seeds.

(Long pause.)

ROE. Stew ready yet?

BELL. Probably not

ROE. I'm hungry

BELL. So am I.

> *(Long pause. **BELL** walks around the room, inspecting this and that.)*

What happened to your grampa?

ROE. Died

BELL. How?

ROE. He was old.

BELL. Huh. I've never met an old man.

ROE. He was...special. He was strong.

BELL. I haven't seen *any* man in – huh. I don't know. Years. I was – small.

ROE. Men die stupid

BELL. That's a fact

ROE. Trying to be big

BELL. Trying to be heroes

ROE. ...Weren't many to start with

BELL. Oh there used to be – just as many as women. Lots more.

ROE. I don't remember it

BELL. Neither do I

ROE. Then how d'you know?

BELL. My mother told me...it was...before the big war. Mostly men fought in that war, is how they died. and I – read books. There are lots of books about men.

ROE. Books.

BELL. I live in a...a library

ROE. *(Never heard this word before.)* A...Library.

BELL. A place in the city that's...big and made of stone, to protect from the bad rain. And...it's filled with books.

ROE. I have a book!

> *(**ROE** gets the book. It's a battered holy bible.)*

BELL. *(This is a phrase she read in a book.)* Are you...a believer?

ROE. It's old.

> *(**BELL** flips open to the first page and sees handwritten inscriptions. When she reads dates, she does it like this: "one-nine-nine-six." There is no reason for her to know to do it another way.)*

BELL. "Clarence Moore, born 1968, died 2047

married to Sarah Winston, 1987, died 2055

Barbara Winston Moore, born 1989, died 2055

married to Patrick Harris, 2014, died 2055

Geena Winston Moore, born 1993, died 2055

married to Theodore Baldwin, 2020, died 2055

Winston C. Moore, /born 1996"

ROE. Winston! That's my Grampa!

BELL. It's a...family history. Of your family.

ROE. What are the numbers?

BELL. ...Time, I think. People used to mark time. With numbers.

ROE. Oh.

BELL. Do you want me to keep reading?

ROE. Yes.

BELL. "...Married to Lucy Johnson 2022, died 2055

Rosie Johnson Moore, born 2026, died 2055

Amber Johnson Moore, born 2029 ...died

married to Don Walsh 2052, died

Ash, born 2056 or 2057, died

Clare, born later, died

Roe, born last"

ROE. That's me! I'm Roe! I'm in the book!

BELL. You didn't know?

ROE. No one told me

BELL. You can't read?

ROE. So?

BELL. Do you want me to teach you?

ROE. What for.

BELL. For...for stories I guess. For...something to do other than...eat and sleep and...try not to die.

ROE. I like eating

BELL. Of course

ROE. I'm hungry

BELL. ...Yes. So am I

ROE. Stew ready yet?

BELL. ...Maybe

(**BELL** *goes to look at it. She pokes the stew with a long-handled fork.*)

We could eat it, but the meat's tough

ROE. Meat's always tough

BELL. It might get more tender if we cook it longer

ROE. The meat's always tough

BELL. (*Sighing.*) OK. Fine.

(**ROE** *brings two bowls and spoons and* **BELL** *drops some food in each one. They eat. They chew. They chew.*)

My name is Bell.

(**ROE** *looks at her.*)

Your name is Roe. My name is Bell. I know your name, now you know mine. Fair trade.

ROE. Bell.

BELL. Yes.

ROE. OK. It's fair.

(*They chew. They chew. They goddamn chew.*)

BELL. Meat's tough.

ROE. –

BELL. What kind of animal is this?

ROE. An old one.

(**BELL** *lets that sink in. Hoping she's wrong.*)

BELL. ...Where did you find an old animal?

(**ROE** *looks at her as if she's stupid.*)

ROE. He was old. I had to.

BELL. You mean –

ROE. I had to.

> (*Long pause.* **BELL** *looks at her food in disgust...then she eats it.*)

BELL. Did...was it him that read the bible?

> (**ROE** *holds in her silence a wailing pain. Yes he did. No words for this feeling. We don't cry here. She takes as long as she needs to get back in control.*)

ROE. Can you read it? He marked the part he liked.

> (**BELL** *opens the bible and finds a corner turned down. She reads.*)

BELL. "For there is hope for a tree,

if it is cut down,

that it will sprout again.

Though its root may grow old in the earth,

and its stump may die in the ground,

yet at the scent of water it will bud

and bring forth branches.

But man dies and is laid away;

he breathes his last

and where is he?

"Oh, that you would hide me in the grave,

that you would conceal me until your wrath is past,

that you would appoint me a set time,

and remember me!"

> (*Long silence. The sound of rain. Lights and sound fade.*)

Later

(It's still raining. **BELL** *lays awake under a blanket on the floor. She watches* **ROE***, asleep in the pile of blankets.* **BELL** *quietly creeps around the cave in the low firelight searching, carefully, slowly. She looks in the chest of clothes, in nooks and crannies, baskets and bags. She tries to move the large rock covering the hole where the meat is kept. It's heavy. She makes as little noise as she can. She hears* **ROE** *stirring and looks over at her, frozen.)*

*(***ROE** *seems to be still asleep.)*

*(***BELL** *removes the men's shirt and wedges it under the rock, trying to move it silently. Finally, almost quietly, she moves it. She tries to look down inside and finds it's too dark to see. Gingerly she lays down on the ground and reaches her arm inside. And reaches. It's deep. She pulls up a small box, opens it, and removes bullets from the box. She returns the box to the hole. She stuffs the bullets in her bra.)*

(Deep breath. She carefully, desperately, re-covers the hole. Brushes dirt off the shirt. Puts it back on. Creeps back to her blanket to sleep.)

Tomorrow

> (**ROE** *makes no effort to be quiet as she stokes the fire, puts water in the pot, pisses in a bucket in the corner.*)

BELL. Is it morning?

ROE. We slept

BELL. ...The rain stopped

ROE. Too soon to go out

BELL. I have to shit

ROE. Can't open the door yet

BELL. Then where do I shit?

ROE. Outside

BELL. You said we can't open the door.

ROE. It's too soon

BELL. OK. Then *where* do I –

ROE. Piss in the bucket. Shit outside.

BELL. But since it's too soon to go outside, what do you expect me to do?

ROE. Wait

BELL. I can't.

ROE. Wait.

> (**BELL** *goes over to the bucket and pisses. She shits.*)

Hey!

> (**BELL** *wipes her ass with her hand and goes to wash her hand in the water bucket.* **ROE** *is pissed.*)

I said we shit outside!

BELL. You weren't going to open the door.

ROE. I kept you alive.

BELL. Maybe. Maybe not.

ROE. You stink

BELL. Shit smells.

I had to. *You* understand "had to." Right?

ROE. –

BELL. I'll bring seeds. When we open the door.

ROE. For the shit?

BELL. For a gun.

ROE. Got no bullets.

BELL. –

ROE. –

BELL. Let's eat.

> *(They put cold stew in bowls. They eat.)*

How long until we can open the door?

ROE. Soon.

> *(Long pause. They eat.)*

BELL. *(Slowly.)* If Pete is hungry...he can eat meat...and if Hazel is hungry, she can eat...what?

ROE. Who's Hazel?

BELL. ... If Pete is hungry...he can eat meat... And if Hazel is hungry, she can eat...Basil.

ROE. *(Wtf is basil?)* Who. Basil.

BELL. If Clare is hungry, she can eat...a pear. And if Jean is hungry, she can eat...? What?

ROE. A pear.

BELL. Think.

ROE. ...It's a game.

BELL. Yes.

    (Pause.)

ROE. I don't know.

BELL. Think.

ROE. –

BELL. *(Fast.)* Pete eats meat. Hazel eats basil. Clare eats a pear. Jean eats –

ROE. – A bean!

BELL. Yes.

ROE. Jean eats a bean!

BELL. If Anne is hungry, she can eat...

ROE. ...Food in a can?

    (From now on the game is very fast.)

BELL. Sure. And if Shelly is hungry...

ROE. Jelly!

BELL. Right. OK. So. If Ryan is hungry, he can *have* –

ROE. – Lion

BELL. No.

ROE. Lion's food.

BELL. No, If Ryan is hungry, he can *have* radishes. But if Bell is hungry, she can *have* beets.

ROE. No.

BELL. Yes. So if Marit is hungry, she can have...?

ROE. Carrots.

BELL. No. But she could have meat.

ROE. No

BELL. Yes. If Chloe was hungry, she could have carrots.

ROE. You changed the rules.

BELL. I made the game.

ROE. That's not fair.

BELL. This is how games work.

ROE. –

BELL. If Tara is hungry she can have...what?

ROE. Tara...Tara, I don't know

BELL. Think.

ROE. AH!

BELL. Tara can have Tomatoes. Sam.

(*Pause.*)

ROE. Sam, Sam, Tara, tomatoes, Sam... S...Stew? Stew.

BELL. Right..

ROE. Roe could have rats.

BELL. Yes.

ROE. Winston could have watermelon!

BELL. Yeah.

ROE. ...That's a good game.

BELL. It's time to open the door.

ROE. Not yet.

BELL. ...I'll come back.

ROE. ...I don't care.

BELL. I'll bring seeds, I want to trade.

ROE. Not yet.

> (**BELL** *sighs. She checks the dryness of her clothes. Good enough. She starts to change her clothes.*)

That shirt is dirty.

> (**BELL** *looks down.*)

BELL. I ran through the woods during a bad rain.

ROE. No. My shirt.

BELL. I slept on the floor.

ROE. –

> (**BELL** *continues to change her clothes.* **ROE** *does pull-ups, or other exercises focused on strength: Push-ups, lunges, that kind of thing.*)

BELL. *(Singing.)*
FEATHERS OF GREEN, FLOWERS OF GOLD,
SINGING DANDY WHERE DID YOU GO?
FOUR CROOKED TREES, SOMEONE GROWS OLD,
SINGING DANDY, WHERE DID YOU GO –

ROE. It got more words.

BELL. What?

ROE. The song

BELL. Yes.

ROE. How?

BELL. I gave it more words.

ROE. Why?

BELL. To help me...remember things.

And for fun, I suppose.

ROE. For fun.

> (**ROE** *shakes her head. Pause.*)

We can open the door now.

BELL. Good.

> (**BELL** *puts on her gas mask.* **ROE** *does the same.* **ROE** *unlocks the multiple locks on the door. She slides the heavy metal door open. Outside it is sunny and bright. Some of the plant life has been killed by the bad rain, withered and blackened, but the big trees, and some bushes with glossy bright colored leaves, still live. They look out.*)

> (*Quick as a flash* **BELL** *grabs a gun from the wall and points it at* **ROE**, *pivoting so her back is to the door.* **ROE** *reaches for her rifle.*)

Don't move.

> (**ROE** *doesn't move.*)

ROE. No bullets.

BELL. That's a lie.

> (*Pause.*)

ROE. That's mine.

BELL. I need it.

ROE. Thief.

> (**BELL** *backs slowly and steadily toward the door, and out, as she speaks.*)

BELL. I'll bring seeds. Soon.

ROE. *You're a goddamn cunt thief!*

BELL. It's a trade. You don't need this many guns. You can spare one. And I'll bring seeds. Tomorrow.

ROE. *(Seething.)* –

> (**BELL** *gets all the way out the door, as far as she can. Then she runs.)*

> (*As soon as* **BELL** *is no longer pointing the gun at* **ROE***,* **ROE** *grabs for her rifle and runs to the door. She points it out the door after* **BELL** *– waits. Waits. Doesn't shoot. Eventually she lowers the gun. She closes the door. She slumps.)*

Tomorrow. Or the Day After

(**ROE** *wears a gas mask. She's geared up with a big bag and the gun. She has her eyes fixed on a particular marshy, grassy spot. She picks her way toward it, avoiding certain spots of earth, and certain big spiky plants.*)

ROE. *(Muttering.)* Poison, poison, sinkhole, poison.

(*A breeze blows one of the spiky plants a little too close to her. Or was it a breeze? She leans away.*)

(Muttering.) Grabby hungry fucker

(*She taunts the plant:*)

Suck air plantfuck

(*The plant...reaches for her? and she avoids it.*)

Ha!

(*She reaches the spot and uses a stick to lift some grasses out of her way. She digs into the grass and lifts up... an empty trap, acid-melted and useless.* **ROE** *pelts it angrily at the ground.*)

(*Then she hears something and crouches down. A moment later we hear it, too. Just a voice:*)

BELL. *(Offstage.)*
FLOWERS OF GOLD...
FOUR CROOKED TREES...
SOMEONE GROWS OLD...
WHERE DID YOU –

Roe?

>(**BELL** *enters wearing a gas mask and carrying the gun.* **ROE** *spies on her.*)

I brought seeds.

>(**BELL** *points the gun.*)

I see you, Roe.

No closer than that.

>(**ROE** *reveals herself, gun pointed.*)

BELL. Put the gun down.

ROE. You first.

BELL. I don't think so.

>*(Pause.)*

I brought seeds.

ROE. You took my gun.

BELL. I had to.

ROE. Give it back.

BELL. No.

ROE. I'll shoot

BELL. You don't want to do that.

ROE. I will though.

BELL. You didn't before and you won't now. You need my help with the plants. You know we can trade for more vegetables, more seeds.

Isn't that right?

ROE. –

BELL. I'm going to count to three and at the same time – at the very same moment – we are going to put down our guns. OK?

ROE. I'll count.

BELL. Fine.

ROE. One. Two. Three.

> *(Neither one of them moves.)*

Go.

> *(Neither one of them moves.)*

BELL. We can start by pointing the guns away from each other. I'll do exactly what you do, exactly when you do it. And you do exactly what I do, when I do it.

ROE. ...A game.

BELL. Yes. We move at exactly the same time.

> *(Long pause. Slowly, slowly, they move their guns a tiny bit. A little more. They mirror each other almost perfectly. They move their arms wide away from their bodies, and crouch to set the guns on the ground. They stand. Is the game over? They reach up to their faces, still in tandem, remove their masks, look at each other. Look up at the sky, deep breath, back at each other. Slowly they step toward each other. They each reach out a hand. When their palms touch the spell breaks.)*

> *(**BELL** draws back her hand as if she's been burned.)*

I brought seeds.

ROE. Give them to me.

(**BELL** *reaches into her bag and removes three small packets.*)

BELL. Here.

(**ROE** *looks at them, sniffs them, opens one and looks inside. Closes it. Pockets the seed packets.*)

Do you want me to show you how to plant them?

ROE. I can do it.

BELL. How deep to put the seeds, how much sun, how much water –

ROE. How much?

BELL. I can show you.

ROE. When?

BELL. Now.

Do you have a box? Off the ground. Filled with fresh clean dirt?

ROE. No

BELL. You'll need that

ROE. Tomorrow

Come tomorrow to show me. I'll have a box.

BELL. OK

(*She backs slowly toward her gun.* **ROE** *does the same. They pick them up at the same time. They each back away, to exit. At the same time they pick up their guns and exit opposite directions.*)

Tomorrow

> (**BELL** *approaches the exterior of* **ROE***'s place.*
> *A big metal door set into the earth, locked*
> *from the outside. Mask on. She takes her*
> *time, looking around. There is a big wooden*
> *box full of dirt, raised up off the ground.*
> **BELL** *inspects the dirt and looks around. She*
> *inspects the locks on the door, tugs on them.*
> *Removes her mask and takes a deep breath.*
> *She bangs on the door.)*

BELL. Roe, it's me.

> (*No response. She tests the weight of the door.*
> *Can she move it? She bangs on the door*
> *again.*)

I'm here to plant seeds!

> (*She keeps trying to lift and shift the door.*
> **ROE** *enters from behind her, wearing her*
> *mask, gun out.*)

ROE. You're making too much noise.

> (**BELL** *turns towards* **ROE**, *hands held*
> *carefully away from her sides to show she*
> *holds no weapon.*)

BELL. I thought you were inside.

ROE. There's creatures around. Hungry.

BELL. You have a gun.

ROE. Not much good when you're ate.

> (*Pause.*)

BELL. Do you patrol the woods every morning?

ROE. Hunting.

BELL. Are you out of meat?

ROE. No.

BELL. OK. Good.

ROE. Don't hit the door.

BELL. Do you want to put that gun down?

ROE. Where's yours?

BELL. I left it behind.

ROE. Stupid.

> (**BELL** *shrugs.*)

Show me.

> (**BELL** *keeps her hands up, turns in a circle.*
> **ROE** *is unconvinced.* **BELL** *lifts up her
> clothes and shows her body. No gun.* **ROE**
> *slowly points the rifle down, then straps it
> across her back. She takes off her mask. Takes
> a deep fearful breath. Relaxes.*)

BELL. Do you want to get the seeds?

> (**ROE** *takes the seeds from her pockets.*)

And clean water? Is it inside?

ROE. There

> (**ROE** *points to a covered bucket sitting under
> the wooden box.*)

BELL. OK. OK so. Let's start with radishes.

We dig a hole...like this (*She digs with her hand.*) one
knuckle deep. Two or three seeds. Cover with the earth.
Pour on some water.

Then one knuckle over is another hole.

ROE. OK.

BELL. You try.

> (**ROE** *digs one.*)

Deeper.

> (**ROE** *does another and another.*)

And now we mark the row.

> (*She produces a small knife from her pocket and places a notch in a twig.* **ROE** *jumps away from her in fear when the knife comes out.* **BELL** *chooses not to notice. She puts the knife away again. She tucks the now-empty seed packet into the notch in the twig and sticks it into the dirt.*)

What's wrong?

ROE. Nothing.

BELL. The packet is labeled, so it's useful. See? R for radish.

ROE. R for radish.

BELL. That's this shape. R.

ROE. R for radish. R for Roe.

BELL. ...Yes.

ROE. Now beans.

BELL. They need a little more space, so we do them on the other edge. We'll put the carrots in the middle.

ROE. Beans need space. Carrots in the middle.

> (**ROE** *begins digging a hole for the beans.* **BELL** *watches.*)

BELL. Deeper. Beans need...yes. And they'll be three knuckles... Yes.

(**ROE** *goes on planting the beans.*)

I also brought...a book.

ROE. A book.

BELL. If you wanted...to learn. To read.

ROE. Read what?

BELL. Books.

ROE. ...You read.

BELL. Don't you want to be able to do it yourself?

ROE. You read.

BELL. Now?

ROE. Yes.

> (**BELL** *produces a slim book from a pocket.*
> **BELL** *begins to read.*)

BELL. "Once there was a wolf and a little girl walking in the woods. The wolf said to the girl: 'what's in that basket?'"

ROE. Wolves don't talk.

BELL. This one does.

ROE. If I heard a wolf talk, I'd kill it.

BELL. OK

ROE. Animals don't talk.

> (**BELL** *aggressively flips the page.*)

BELL. Fine.

"There was a girl. She lived in a cottage with her mother."

> (**BELL** *looks up.*)

Not animals.

(**ROE** *shrugs and keeps planting.*)

..."Each day the girl went into the forest to gather berries, and her mother said 'be home by dark! There are fairies in the trees and if they wish you harm I cannot protect you.'"

ROE. What's fairies?

BELL. Like a person but magic.

ROE. Magic.

BELL. It's...a specialness.

Power.

ROE. Specialness.

(**ROE** *stares at* **BELL**. **BELL** *stares at* **ROE**.)

(**BELL** *reads.*)

BELL. "Each day the girl gathered berries and went home before dark. But one day, she walked into a clearing filled with flowers. The sun was hot, and her basket was heavy, so she laid herself down to sleep."

(**ROE** *snorts.*)

ROE. Outside?

BELL. Yes.

ROE. She'll get ate.

BELL. ...Maybe

(**BELL** *waits.* **ROE** *keeps planting.*)

..."The girl woke and it was dusk. The forest was dark and strange. Then there appeared a creature who shined like starlight and smelled of lemons."

ROE. Lemons!

BELL. Yes.

> (**BELL** *waits*. **ROE** *doesn't say any more.*)

…"The girl knew this was a fairy, but she was not afraid. She offered the fairy some berries to eat. But when the fairy reached out to touch her cheek the girl drew back and said, 'Dear fairy, I must go home or my mother will miss me.'"

"The fairy smiled. 'Since you have given me a gift, I will give one to you.' She waved her hand and the girl was home. In her basket, where there had been blackberries, there were now jewels and gold."

ROE. Bad trade.

BELL. It's a story.

ROE. Can't eat gold.

BELL. It's not real.

ROE. Carrots next.

> (**BELL** *looks up from the book.*)

BELL. You need to water the dirt first. Then just put the seeds in…a fingertip.

ROE. A fingertip.

> (**BELL** *goes to demonstrate.*)

BELL. I'll show you.

ROE. I can do it.

BELL. OK

> (**BELL** *waits.*)

> (**ROE** *looks up.*)

ROE. "Jewels and gold...?"

BELL. You're right. It's a bad trade.

ROE. Read!

> (**BELL** *raises her eyebrows. She reads.*)

BELL. ..."The next night, the girl again stayed in the forest. She called out 'fairy, my friend, I have brought you a gift' and the fairy appeared, smelling of lemons, with a laugh that pealed like a bell."

"The girl offered the fairy strawberries and a warm scarf, but the fairy smiled and said, 'I need no clothes, for I am the same stuff as the earth and I am always just the way I ought to be. But I will eat some berries.' The fairy reached to touch the girl's cheek and again the girl drew back, saying 'my mother will miss me.' The fairy waved her hand and the girl was home, with the scarf transformed into a golden cloak lined with fur."

> (**BELL** *glances at* **ROE**, *who nods approvingly. A cloak is better than gold.*)

"The girl's mother begged her not to test the fairy's friendship. She said, 'you may not be so lucky a third time.'"

"But the girl remembered the smell of lemons. She stayed out the next night until dark, her basket filled with lingonberries and a wooden flute in her hand."

"When the fairy appeared the girl said, 'Fairy, you have been a friend to me. Let me give you one small gift.'"

"And the fairy smiled and ate the lingonberries while the girl played a simple song. The fairy reached out to touch the girl's cheek and this time the girl did not draw back."

> (**ROE** *has finished planting. She watches* **BELL** *as she reads.*)

"The fairy drew the girl into a wild and glorious dance and the girl's heart went one two with her feet as the flute played all on its own. All night they danced until the sky grew bright and the fairy said, 'Come with me into the fairy realm and be my darling and you will live to dance ten thousand nights.' But the girl kissed the fairy and said, 'I cannot, for my mother will miss me.'"

"So the fairy was filled with wrath. She snapped her fingers and the girl returned home with empty hands, her feet torn and bloody. The girl's mother wept, but the girl remembered that night always with joy and longing."

"When her feet healed, the girl returned to the forest. She called to the fairy, 'My friend! My friend!' but no answer came. In the morning, the girl found in her hand her lost flute, which had turned to gold."

"Whenever she played it she thought of the fairy and her heart was glad to know she had once had a true friend who loved her still."

...That's the end.

ROE. I like it.

BELL. ...It's just a story.

ROE. A good story.

> (**ROE** *looks at* **BELL**. *Suddenly* **ROE** *leans in and buries her face in* **BELL**'s *hair, smelling her.* **BELL** *is surprised but does not move away.*)

What do lemons smell like?

BELL. ...I don't know. Good.

> (**ROE** *nods. Of course.*)

Do you want to keep this?

(She holds out the book.)

ROE. For trade.

BELL. It's a gift.

> *(**ROE** takes the book and pockets it. Pause.)*

> *(**ROE** goes and opens her door, unlocking each of the three big locks.)*

> *(She jerks her head for **BELL** to follow her inside.)*

> *(She takes a can from the wall of cans and opens it, splitting the contents between two bowls.)*

> *(She hands one bowl to **BELL**.)*

> *(**BELL** looks at the label on the can.)*

Peaches!

ROE. You like peaches?

BELL. ...I've never had one.

> *(**BELL** picks one out of the bowl with her fingers and takes a bite. It is amazing. She savors it. Then she wolfs down the rest of her peaches in a few huge bites.)*

ROE. You like it.

BELL. Yes.

> *(Pause. **BELL** appraises the wall of cans.)*

...How many cans do you have there, you think?

ROE. A lot.

BELL. There have to be at least... *(Quick math.)* two thousand cans. Maybe more. That's...years. Five, six years, if you eat one every day.

ROE. –

BELL. You never counted?

ROE. What for?

BELL. To know...how long you have.

ROE. There's meat. Beans and carrots soon.

I only eat the cans when I need to.

BELL. Like right now?

ROE. Today's special.

BELL. Why?

ROE. ...Grampa passed. Forty days ago.

BELL. ...That's hard.

ROE. "Forty days and forty nights."

BELL. Before that...it was you and him?

ROE. And my sister. Clare.

But she got killed by a bear. Two summers ago.

BELL. –

ROE. We ate that bear thirty-six days.

BELL. ...My mother passed six winters ago. And my sister went last summer. I've been alone since then.

ROE. Not alone now.

BELL. ...I don't mind. I have the books. The sun and birds.

ROE. And me.

> (**BELL** *looks at* **ROE**. *Suddenly very very tense.*)

BELL. You never know how things will go.

> (*Pause.* **ROE** *looks away.*)

ROE. Gotta fix the fire.

> (**ROE** *walks over to the fire with her back to* **BELL**. **BELL** *silently slips the gun from her pocket and advances slowly toward* **ROE**'s *back.* **ROE** *suddenly bows her head.*)

I gotta...

> (**BELL** *freezes. Gun behind her back.* **ROE** *doesn't turn around yet.*)

After Clare died, Grampa writ her in the book.

> (**ROE** *turns to look at* **BELL**.)

But after Grampa died...No one writ for him.

BELL. Do you want me to –?

ROE. ...Please.

> (*Pause.*)

BELL. OK.

> (**ROE** *gets the book. When she's not looking* **BELL** *slips the gun back into her pocket.* **BELL** *writes.*)

Winston. "Died, later."

ROE. Good

> (*Pause.*)

Put you in the book.

BELL. I'm not your family.

ROE. You're the only person I know.

BELL. I don't belong in your book.

> (**ROE** *takes the pencil and shakily writes a "B".*)

ROE. "B" for Beans. "B" for Bell.

BELL. *(Sighs.)* Yes.

ROE. Then.

BELL. "E"

> *(She points to another E in the book.)*

Like that one.

ROE. And then.

BELL. "L"

> *(She points.)*

Two "L"s.

> (**ROE** *copies it down.*)

ROE. There.

BELL. You shouldn't have done that.

ROE. I can do what I want. It's my book.

BELL. Maybe you'll change your mind and not want me in the book.

ROE. ...Maybe.

> (**ROE** *returns the book to its spot. While her back is turned,* **BELL** *pockets two cans – one in each pocket.* **ROE** *returns.*)

BELL. It's getting late. I better go.

ROE. ...You could stay.

BELL. No. I can't.

ROE. Why not.

BELL. I'll come back. Tomorrow.

> (**BELL** *dons her gas mask and exits.* **ROE** *watches her go. She closes and locks the door.*)

Tomorrow

(**BELL** *stands in the doorway of* **ROE**'s *place.*
She pulls off her mask.)

BELL. I brought beans and radishes. And herbs.

ROE. Herbs?

BELL. For more flavor. In the stew. If you...want to make
stew.

ROE. ...Gotta check my traps.

BELL. OK.

(**ROE** *exits.*)

(**BELL** *hangs around the shelter. She wanders,*
looks at things. She pockets two more cans of
food. She pockets a candle. She starts slicing
up the vegetables.)

(**ROE** *returns.*)

Anything?

ROE. A...this

(**ROE** *holds up an unrecognizable animal*
carcass. Might be a squirrel except it's big.
Might be a rabbit except it has a long tail.
Might be a possum except it's definitely not
a possum.)

BELL. You sure that's safe to eat?

ROE. No.

BELL. –

ROE. Guess it's a game.

(**BELL** *laughs.*)

BELL. I guess it is.

> (**ROE** *skins the animal.* **BELL** *pours water in the pot. Adds the veggies. Pause. She adds the herbs.*)

ROE. Where do you live?

BELL. I told you. A library.

ROE. But where?

BELL. In the city

ROE. But. Where?

BELL. *(Hard.)* In the city

ROE. I wanna see your place

BELL. No

ROE. You've seen my place. I want to see yours. Fair trade.

BELL. ...Maybe. Sometime. Not yet.

ROE. Why not?

BELL. It's a far walk.

ROE. You walked here.

BELL. Maybe. Not yet.

ROE. –

BELL. It's just...

ROE. –

BELL. Sometime. Sometime you can see my place.

ROE. When?

BELL. Soon.

ROE. When?

BELL. In...three days. You can come. To my place in three days. You can...look at the books.

ROE. Can't read 'em.

BELL. You're learning the letters.

ROE. ...slowly.

BELL. We can practice more today. If you want.

ROE. ...Maybe.

BELL. –

ROE. Do another. From the book.

BELL. Put the meat in the pot.

ROE. And then you can read.

BELL. ...OK

> (**ROE** *drops the meat in the pot. She turns to*
> **BELL** *like "well?"* **BELL** *picks up the book. She*
> *flips through it.)*

"Once there was a golden city filled with people. The city was large and had twisting golden streets, and down every street was a marvelous bakery, hatmaker's or oddity's shop."

ROE. What? What. "Filled with people?"

BELL. There used to be more.

ROE. Like...fifty?

BELL. Millions. More.

ROE. No.

> (**BELL** *shrugs.)*

"Oddity shop?"

BELL. It used to be different.

The world.

You could go to a building and buy things.

ROE. Food?

BELL. ...I think so.

ROE. Food in cans?!

BELL. Yes.

But also things you just...like. Pretty things. Books.

> (**ROE** *laughs. This is made up.*)

Truly.

> (**ROE** *frowns.*)

ROE. They all died.

BELL. Yes.

ROE. "Filled with people..."

> (**BELL** *and* **ROE** *think about a place that is filled with people.*)

> (**BELL** *closes the book.*)

Read.

BELL. I don't want to read right now.

ROE. Read!

BELL. I said no.

> (**ROE** *huffs and bangs around the room.*)

> (**BELL** *waits.*)

ROE. ...Why not.

BELL. It makes me sad.

ROE. Why?

BELL. Don't you feel sad that all the people in the world are dead?

ROE. *(Scoffs.)* I'm not dead. You're not dead.

BELL. Don't you feel sad that the world is so different from the book?

(**ROE** *shrugs.*)

ROE. It's just a story.

BELL. ...Yes.

ROE. ...A good story.

BELL. You like the book.

ROE. Yes!

BELL. But you don't understand it.

ROE. I understand! I'm not stupid.

BELL. But you've never heard about cities, or people, or bakeries, or...

ROE. You can tell me.

BELL. Why didn't your grampa tell you?

ROE. ...Grampa.

Did not like to talk very much.

BELL. So very different from you.

(**ROE** *looks at* **BELL** *like she's nuts.*)

...It's a joke.

ROE. Grampa didn't like other people too much.

...

...He wouldn't like a city filled with people.

BELL. ...How many people have you met?

ROE. I've met you.

BELL. Who else?

(**ROE** *shrugs.*)

How many that you didn't kill?

(**ROE** *shrugs.*)

I've met seven people.

ROE. In the city?

They live at the library?

BELL. No. They're all gone I think.

All dead.

(**ROE** *nods. Of course they are.*)

(*She sets about doing some kind of household task, like patching a pair of pants.*)

ROE. Stew ready yet?

BELL. Almost certainly not.

ROE. Hmph.

(*Long pause.*)

BELL. If you like the book why not learn to read it yourself?

ROE. I'm learning the letters.

BELL. ...You don't really want to.

ROE. ... I like when you read.

BELL. I might not always be around to read to you. Don't you want to be able to read when I'm not here?

ROE. ...Where are you going?

BELL. ...I live far away.

Sometimes you're here and I'm not here.

ROE. But you'll come back.

BELL. What if I die?

ROE. Are you going to die?

BELL. ...No.

ROE. Alright.

> *(Long pause.)*

I like when you read.

BELL. Are you scared of being alone?

ROE. ...No. But I like being not-alone better.

BELL. ...Me too.

> *(Long pause.)*

Are you scared to die?

ROE. ...No and yes.

BELL. –

ROE. Not scared to be dead. Just...I don't want to hurt.

BELL. ...You're scared of pain.

> *(**ROE** shrugs.)*

ROE. Aren't you?

BELL. What?

ROE. Scared of pain?

> *(Short pause.)*

BELL. No.

ROE. Why not?

BELL. Pain is...all the time. I don't want to be scared all the time.

ROE. But you're scared to die.

BELL. I don't want to be dead.

ROE. Everything dies.

BELL. Can't be sure of that 'til it's proved.

> (**ROE** gives **BELL** a searching look.)

ROE. Stew ready yet?

> (**BELL** sighs.)

BELL. Maybe. Why don't you check?

> (**ROE** looks at the stew. She pokes it.)

ROE. I'm hungry.

BELL. OK...let's eat.

> (**ROE** cheerily dishes up the stew into bowls.)
>
> (She sits and begins ravenously eating.)
>
> (Long pause.)
>
> (**ROE** scratches at her neck.)
>
> (She scratches at her chest.)
>
> (She looks at **BELL**.)

ROE. Why aren't you eating?

BELL. I am

> (**ROE** scratches her back.)

ROE. You're not.

BELL. I'm eating slowly.

ROE. You're not.

BELL. OK.

I'm not.

ROE. Why not.

BELL. I think…it's not safe.

> (**ROE** *sets down her bowl.*)

ROE. Why do you think that?

> (*Pause.* **ROE** *is itching and scratching, all over her body. It's getting a little wild.*)

Bell. Why do you think it's not safe.

BELL. The herbs I put in. They grow by a pond. I've seen animals eat it and they…they died.

ROE. Why'd you put them in, then?

BELL. I thought… I should take your food.

I need your food.

> (**ROE**'*s itching and scratching is getting more and more aggressive. She takes off her shirt to reach.*)

ROE. Plenty for both of us.

BELL. No

ROE. There is

BELL. Not forever. I want to grow old.

ROE. Alone?

BELL. I can live alone. I can't live hungry.

> (**ROE** *itching and scratching furiously. She wants to lash out but it hurts and itches too much and she can't stop scratching.* **ROE** *is furious and betrayed. She almost starts to cry [we don't cry here]. She wails and scratches and falls to the ground scratching but she doesn't cry.*)

ROE. Cunt.

Cunt cunt cunt cunt.

> (**BELL** *is sorry. She almost starts to cry [we don't cry here].*)

BELL. I'm sorry. I'm sorry it hurts you.

I wish I could take it back.

We could maybe have...

Probably not.

> (**ROE** *is scratching big long welts in her skin. It bleeds. It's horrible. There's blood on the ground and on her hands and arms and face.*)

Oh no, no, that's too – don't do that it's horrible.

ROE. Itches. Gotta scratch it.

Your fault!

AAAaaauuuugghhhh!!!!!

BELL. Yes, it's my fault.

ROE. I'm not going to die.

BELL. You are though.

> (**ROE** *shoves her fingers down her throat and forces herself to throw up into the pot of stew.*)

ROE. Why would you do that why would you why...what the goddamn

> (**ROE** *dashes over to the clean water bucket and begins chugging water furiously.* **BELL** *just watches.* **ROE** *vomits again. She chugs more water.*)

BELL. What's the point living for a while if we're just going to die?

ROE. Point?

BELL. I want to keep going until I see what happens next

ROE. What happens next? What?

BELL. Something has to happen. Something else. Other than just...this again, and again, food and...more food, and...again someone dies and I watch and I think... Something better might happen. If I live long enough to see it.

> (**ROE** *pours the water over her head, over her bleeding skin.*)

ROE. So what?

BELL. What do you mean?

ROE. You live long, see something nice. You gonna tell someone about it? There won't be anyone to tell.

BELL. I'll just...see it.

> (**ROE** *itches and scratches. She bleeds. She washes her wounds and scratches some more and bleeds some more and drinks more water.*)

I'm sorry.

ROE. Cunt.

> (**ROE** *dips the rag in water. She rubs it on her scratches. She fetches a jar of ointment that is sitting on a shelf. She rubs it on her scratches. She sighs. She tries to stop herself from scratching and somewhat succeeds.*)

...Maybe this is what happens next.

BELL. What?

ROE. You murder me and I don't die.

You can tell me about that.

I'll listen.

You read the books.

I'll listen.

That's something.

That's better than just not dying.

BELL. That's...[sweet]

Aren't you going to try to kill me back?

ROE. –

> (**ROE** *keeps bathing her scratches.*)

BELL. I'm sorry I murdered you.

ROE. I'm not dead.

BELL. Not yet.

ROE. Nope.

> (*Long pause.*)

I think maybe you're crazy.

BELL. Who gets to decide that?

ROE. I do.

BELL. Well I don't agree. I think I'm...a person who is going to live.

ROE. Unless I kill you.

> (**BELL** *puts her hand to her pocket. Maybe there is a gun there. She doesn't draw it.*)

BELL. Are you going to try?

ROE. ...Not right now.

(**BELL** *doesn't believe her.*)

You're the only person.

(**BELL** *doesn't believe her.*)

I don't want to be alone.

(**BELL** *relaxes only slightly.*)

BELL. OK.

ROE. I'm not going to kill you.

BELL. OK. Me neither.

(**ROE** *keeps putting ointment on her scratches.*)

Let me do that.

(**BELL** *puts ointment on* **ROE**'s *scratches.* **ROE** *tenses up but lets her. Long pause.*)

ROE. I wanted...want...wanted to give you things.

BELL. I know.

ROE. Don't you want to give me things?

(*Long pause.*)

BELL. ...I want to tell you a story.

ROE. From the book?

BELL. No.

ROE. ...OK

(**ROE** *waits expectantly. Pause.*)

BELL. Once there were three women. A family. They lived together and they loved each other and they were happy when they sang and laughed together, but they were also angry and afraid because there wasn't enough food. Then one of them died and the other two were so sad. They cried and they sang sad songs but with only two of them there was more food, so secretly they were also happy. They both were happy, but they tried to keep the happiness secret from each other because they felt guilty and they felt ashamed.

And time wore on and the food got less. There were mistakes. A bad rain. The happiness got less, too.

Then another one of them died, and the one who was left alive was so sad because now she was alone. But she was happy, too, because before she was always hungry and now she was less hungry. And she was also happy because she discovered that she didn't feel any guilt. She didn't feel any shame.

She didn't have to keep secrets anymore. And there was still the sun, and the birds, and books, and little yellow flowers. And she found she could still sing and she could still laugh, all by herself.

ROE. –

BELL. That's the story

ROE. I don't like it

BELL. OK

> (*Long pause.* **ROE** *has mostly stopped scratching.*)

ROE. Who will remember you if you are the last one, all alone?

BELL. Why would I care about that after I'm gone?

ROE. Grampa always...he said, remember me, remember me.

BELL. And you do. Does it make him less dead?

> (*Pause.*)

ROE. Sometimes I feel like he's here.

BELL. He's not.

ROE. –

BELL. If you were smart. If you wanted to live. You'd kill me. Find my place. Take my garden. Never let another person in your place. Never trust another person not to kill you. Save your cans. Try to...get old.

ROE. Grampa never did say I was smart.

BELL. –

ROE. My sister was smart. Real smart.

I remember her, too.

> *(Long pause.)*

BELL. ...You have a sweet heart.

ROE. –

BELL. I'm sorry I made you itch and hurt.

> *(Pause.)*

ROE. You gonna try to kill me again?

> *(Pause.)*

BELL. I don't know.

> *(Pause.)*

ROE. You like me?

BELL. I do like you

ROE. Alright.

> *(They sit quietly by the fire.* **BELL** *puts ointment on* **ROE***'s skin.)*
>
> *(The fire dies down and lights slowly fade.)*

Three Days Later

(The city. **ROE** *wanders the streets, shout-singing. Mask on.)*

ROE.

"LITTLE YELLOW FLOWERS, DANDY, DANDY, WHERE DID YOU GO?

Where are you Bell?

LOOKING FOR A LIBRARY SOMEWHERE IN THE CITY, WHERE DID YOU GO?"

BELL! Bell!!!!

*(***ROE*** *wanders. She doesn't like the city. She likes the forest much better.)*

*(***BELL*** *comes running out lightly dressed, gas mask on, grabs* **ROE***'s hand without a word and pulls her away.)*

BELL. *(Whispering.)* Shut up, cunt, shut up, shut up, shut up

*(***BELL*** *pulls* **ROE** *off, into the library where* **BELL** *lives.)*

(It is a small square room with walls made of bookshelves. Sunlight filters in between the books.)

(A sofa in one corner with a blanket where **BELL** *sleeps. A bucket of water. A small table.)*

(Underneath are two empty tin cans. A bin with one radish and a tiny handful of beans inside.)

(They remove their masks. **ROE** *has partially healed scratches on her arms and face.)*

What the hell are you doing here.

ROE. You said I could come in three days. I'm here.

BELL. That was before I murdered you!

ROE. I'm not dead.

BELL. How do you know I'm not going to murder you again right now?

ROE. Are you?

(Pause.)

BELL. Not *right* now.

ROE. OK.

BELL. OK. So this is my place. You've seen it. Get out.

ROE. Where are your plants?

BELL. On the roof.

ROE. Where's your food?

BELL. The plants are on the roof.

ROE. Your other food.

BELL. –

ROE. Where'd you get those cans.

BELL. ...I found them.

ROE. Just yesterday?

BELL. Might've been.

ROE. Or was it three days ago. At my place.

BELL. No.

ROE. Then where'd you find 'em?

BELL. You're not the only person who ever found food cans.

ROE. ...I s'pose not.

(Pause.)

BELL. What do you want?

ROE. I brought meat. To trade.

BELL. For what.

ROE. ...Carrots.

BELL. I don't have any carrots right now.

ROE. Beans.

BELL. That's all my beans.

(She gestures to the nearly empty bin.)

Waiting for more to grow.

ROE. Radishes.

BELL. –

ROE. ...Books, then.

BELL. Books.

ROE. I need another book.

BELL. You don't know how to read the first book.

ROE. Give me a book.

BELL. Why do you want a book?

ROE. I want one.

BELL. Why?

ROE. To have.

BELL. –

ROE. Give me a book. I brought meat to trade.

BELL. What book?

ROE. Any book.

Three books.

BELL. ...Two.

ROE. Two big books.

BELL. OK.

> (**BELL** *wanders around the room, touching the spines of the books like lovers and friends. She pulls a few off the shelf, looks at them, puts them back. This is a big decision.*)

BELL. This one. Stories. Animals that talk.

ROE. Animals don't talk.

> (**BELL** *puts it back.*)

BELL. Poetry.

ROE. What?

BELL. Pretty words. Like the Holy Bible.

ROE. Already got one.

BELL. Then what do you want?

ROE. ...Pictures.

> (*Pause.*)

BELL. Pictures.

> (**BELL** *exits.* **ROE** *looks around. She sniffs the cans suspiciously. She touches everything. She studies the nearly-empty food bin.* **BELL** *returns with a large art book and a* Vogue *September Issue.*)

What about these?

(**ROE** *is speechless.* **ROE** *turns the pages and stares and stares at the pictures.*)

Good? Is it a trade?

ROE. It's not fair.

BELL. You said two big books.

ROE. I need to give you more meat.

BELL. ...OK. I'll come get it. Maybe...tomorrow.

(**ROE** *places a packet of meat on the table.*)

(*She takes the books in her arms.*)

ROE. Tomorrow.

(**ROE** *exits.* **BELL** *picks up the packet of meat. She smells it. She rips it open and begins to eat the meat raw, ravenously. After a few bites, she stops. Wraps it back up like it's precious.*)

(*She makes a decision.*)

Not Tomorrow. The Day After Tomorrow

>*(Inside **ROE**'s place. **ROE** is asleep. The fire has
>dwindled through the night. Loud banging at
>the door. From outside we hear **BELL**'s voice.)*

BELL. *(Offstage.)* Roe! Let me in! Roe, the frost! Open the
door!

>*(**ROE** wakes up groggy and bewildered.)*

Let me in! The frost!

>*(**ROE** gets up and goes to the door. She grabs
>her gun. She unlocks the three inside locks
>and opens the door. **BELL** is outside, bundled
>up top to toe. Mask on. It is very very early
>morning. A sudden frost has descended. A
>foot of snow has fallen in the night. It is
>terribly cold.)*

Your beans will die in the cold. You have to bring them
inside. NOW.

>*(**ROE** drops her gun and dashes outside,
>leaving the door wide open. **BELL** steps quickly
>inside. She takes hold of the door and begins
>trying to pull it closed. It's heavy. She pulls it
>slowly, inch by inch. **ROE** comes huffing back,
>pulling the box. **BELL** keeps trying to close the
>door until **ROE** steps through it with the box.
>She is partway through the door when the
>legs of the box catch.)*

ROE. Help.

>*(**BELL** pauses momentarily, then helps pull
>the box through. **ROE** quickly finishes closing
>the door and locks it up. She sits down,
>huffing and rubbing her cold limbs.)*

You were closing the door.

BELL. It's so cold.

> (**BELL** *removes an outer layer or two of clothing. She goes to the fire to warm her hands.*)

ROE. You saved my beans.

BELL. Maybe.

> (*Pause.*)

ROE. ..."Come with me into the fairy realm and be my darling and you will live to dance ten thousand nights."

> (**BELL** *looks at* **ROE**. *She is surprised. Touched.*)

ROE. I like that. I like the pictures. I like you.

BELL. I tried to kill you.

ROE. ...You're the only person.

> (*Pause.*)

BELL. I like you, too.

ROE. ...Hungry?

BELL. I have nothing to trade.

ROE. It's yours. For the books.

> (**ROE** *goes to the chiller and pulls out a packet of meat.* **BELL** *watches her.*)

BELL. Is it...

ROE. Squirrel. Not so tough.

BELL. Oh. Good.

(**ROE** *places the meat on a spit over the fire.
They sit near the fire, warming.*)

ROE. Read. Please.

BELL. Read what?

ROE. The story. The fairy. From your book.

BELL. It's your book.

(**ROE** *picks up the book and hands it to* **BELL**.)

"There was a girl. She lived in a cottage" –

ROE. Not that part!

BELL. What?

ROE. Later. "But the girl remembered the smell of lemons."

BELL. ...OK.

(**BELL** *flips to a new page. She reads.*)

"But the girl remembered the smell of lemons. She
stayed out the next night until dark, her basket filled
with lingonberries and a wooden flute in her hand."

(**ROE** *sighs a happy sigh.*)

"When the fairy appeared the girl said, 'Fairy, you have
been a friend to me'...

...The fairy reached out to touch the girl's cheek and
this time the girl did not draw back."

(**ROE** *leans in closer.*)

"The fairy drew the girl into a wild and glorious dance
and the girl's heart went one two with her feet. All
night they danced, until the fairy said, 'Come with me
into the fairy realm and be my darling and you will live
to dance ten thousand nights.'"

(**BELL**'s *voice cracks on the last line.* **ROE** *looks at her.*)

"But the girl kissed the fairy and said" –

(**ROE** *kisses* **BELL**. **BELL** *drops the book. They kiss and touch and fall desperately into each other. Thunk. A knife has slipped out of* **BELL**'s *pocket and fallen to the floor.*)

(**ROE** *stops at the noise. She looks down at the knife.*)

ROE. What's that?

BELL. It was in my pocket. It must have...fallen out.

(**ROE** *looks at* **BELL**. *She reaches for her gun, a step or two away. Instantly* **BELL** *reaches in her pocket for the handgun and shoots* **ROE**, *who falls down. She lays there in pooling blood, clutching her side.* **BELL** *is shaky and upset, but she keeps her cool.*)

I'm...sorry. Sorry it hurts. I wish I was better at – so it wouldn't hurt.

(*She kneels beside* **ROE**, *softly stroking* **ROE**'s *cheek. She kisses* **ROE** *on the forehead.*)

I'll write you. In the book.

I just... I need your food.

ROE. Your garden –

BELL. My garden is dead

I need yours

ROE. I gave it –

I would have –

(**BELL** *nearly cries but she doesn't.*)

BELL. It's not enough for two.

> (**ROE** *stares. Not surprised. Heartbroken. Suddenly she lunges toward* **BELL** *and grabs her throat.* **BELL** *pokes* **ROE** *in the eyes.* **ROE** *jerks back and* **BELL** *wriggles away.* **ROE** *pulls* **BELL** *back by the hair. She grabs the nearest thing – the metal stewpot. She bashes* **BELL** *in the face. Again. Again.)*

ROE. Bell?

> (**BELL** *is dead. [We don't cry here].)*

> (**ROE** *goes to the poker still sitting over the fire and holds it against her gunshot wound to cauterize it. Deep breath. She sits next to* **BELL**'s *body, humming the song.)*

ROE.

"DANDY, WHERE DID YOU GO…HMM HMM"

> (*She gently runs her fingers through* **BELL**'s *bloody hair.)*

Tomorrow

(**ROE** *walks alone along the path wearing a gas mask. There is snow and ice piled on the ground in drifts. The sound of tricking water. Ice melt.*)

(*On the path, small yellow flowers peek through the snow.* **ROE** *stops and looks at the flowers. She takes a deep breath. She takes off her mask. She looks up at the sky and feels the breeze on her face. The sound of birds.*)

ROE. ...The sun is bright.

...Somewhere there are birds.

...Feel the breeze. The sweat on your skin.

...Taste the air. Perfume. Yellow flowers.

This is the world without a mask.

It will kill you.

...But the girl remembered the smell of lemons.

...Be my darling and you will live to dance ten thousand nights.

End of Play

www.ingramcontent.com/pod-product-compliance
Lightning Source LLC
Chambersburg PA
CBHW070350120726
47909CB00008B/2794